R.L. STINE

INTERIOR ILLUSTRATIONS BY DAVID FEBLAND

LOOK FOR THESE TWISTAPLOT® BOOKS
BY R.L. STINE

Horrors of the Haunted Museum

Coming soon:

Golden Sword of Dragonwalk

ISBN 0-590-48555-5

12 11 10 9 8 7 6 5 4 3 2 1   1   5 6 7 8 9/9 0/0

Printed in the U.S.A.   40

BEWARE!!!

DO NOT READ
THIS BOOK
FROM
BEGINNING TO END

You are about to climb into the *Time Raider*, an amazing machine that will carry you through the dimension of time, but *only* if you follow the directions at the bottom of each page. Think carefully before you flip a page. A wrong turn could mean danger or even death. The right one could make you a hero.

What happens depends on you. If you get into trouble, turn back and choose a different way out. If you're having a good time, keep going!

Time travel is always dangerous. It calls for clear thinking and quick decisions. If you make the right moves, you can enjoy dozens of adventures into the past and future — and get back home safely. If you make the wrong moves, you could be lost in time, trapped in the pages of this book — *forever!*

Good luck — and safe travels!

Now turn to PAGE 2.

A weekend visit to your Uncle Edgar's is always exciting. His old house is filled with rooms to explore; rooms cluttered with old furniture and toys, strange books and magazines, and weird objects and machines. Uncle Edgar is an inventor, and you never know what kind of invention you're going to find him working on.

"Come in, come in," Uncle Edgar says, ushering you into his lab. "I want to show you my greatest creation ever!"

"That's what you said about your last creation," you say. "Remember — the underwater pop-up toaster for deep-sea divers who like a big breakfast?"

"Forget about that," Uncle Edgar says, taking you up to a large metal capsule with two seats and a giant control panel inside. "Just take a look at this marvel of mine! This is the *Time Raider*. It's a time machine!"

You look at the giant capsule carefully. "All this machinery just to tell what time it is?" you ask.

Your uncle is in no mood for your teasing. "You and I are going to travel through time," he says seriously. He pushes you inside the Time Raider and climbs in after you. "What adventures we will have!" he says, turning knobs.

You know in your heart that the whole thing is silly. But he's so excited, you don't want to spoil his fun. "Here, put this on," he says. He hands you a green pendant on a silver chain. You put it around your neck.

"If you get into trouble," he warns, "just

squeeze the green pendant. No matter where you are, it will return you to the time machine. I'm wearing one, too."

You watch as he pushes buttons and turns knobs. The control panel lights up, and the whole capsule begins to hum and shake. "We're off!" Uncle Edgar shouts. "We're moving! I can feel it! Oh, wait a minute!" He jumps out of his seat and climbs out of the time machine. "I forgot my glasses! Be right back!"

The door slams behind him. "Wait!" you cry. "Uncle Edgar, the machine . . . it's . . ." You realize to your horror that the Time Raider is no longer in the lab. Suddenly you are surrounded by whirling red-and-yellow lights. Stars seem to whiz by. Uncle Edgar has been left behind. You are on your own — the first person ever to travel through time.

Your eyes dart across the blinking control board. You see two large, orange buttons. One says FORWARD, the other says BACKWARD.

Shall you visit the past — or the future?

This is your first big decision.

If you choose to visit the past, turn to PAGE 4.
If you choose to visit the future, turn to PAGE 8.

You push the button marked BACKWARD and close your eyes. You feel the Time Raider jolt, then bounce, then shake. Your trip backward in time seems to take less than a second. Did Uncle Edgar's invention work at all?

You look out through the doorway, expecting to see the familiar insides of your uncle's lab. But the machine has definitely moved you somewhere. You look out onto a dark green forest of trees and tangled shrubs. A robin sings in a branch above your head. A squirrel with a burr on its tail hops past the time machine uncertainly.

Should you get out and explore? The surroundings don't look very exciting. But maybe you have traveled back to an earlier North America, a continent of wilderness and natural beauty.

You must decide whether to explore this forest or go farther back in time.

If you choose to go out and explore, turn to PAGE 10.

If you choose to go back farther in time, push the button once and turn to PAGE 6.

If you wish to go a lot farther back in time, push the button twice and turn to PAGE 25.

This time, the Time Raider gives you more than a split-second jolt. It shakes and whirs, and a rainbow of colors shoots past your eyes. You feel as though you are spinning backward, then tumbling as you spin. When the capsule finally lands, your head spins for another few minutes, and you have trouble keeping your balance.

Soon, however, you begin to feel like yourself. You look out the doorway. A thick layer of untouched snow covers the ground beneath a bright blue sky. The machine has brought you to a scene of sparkling, wintry beauty. You search the small capsule and — sure enough! — Uncle Edgar remembered to pack a down coat and wool hat for you.

Cautiously, you poke open the capsule door. You can hear children's voices in the distance. A blast of cold air feels refreshing on your face as you pull the cap down over your ears and look around.

You have landed next to a woodshed at the side of a steep, snow-covered hill. A few yards behind the woodshed is a large, old-fashioned-looking house. Smoke floats up from its chimney, and the aroma of hot apple pie has somehow mingled with the smell of the burning wood from the fireplace beneath the chimney.

At the foot of the hill, two boys about your age are arguing about the flimsy wooden sled at their feet. The boys are wearing leggings and gray wool sweaters, black caps, and black rubber boots. "They look like the boys in Uncle Edgar's old photo album," you tell yourself. You creep around to the side of the woodshed to hear what the boys are saying.

"Of course it won't steer, Edgar. That new rudder you invented just doesn't work!" the smaller boy is saying heatedly.

Edgar? Invented? Can that boy actually be your Uncle Edgar? Have you traveled back forty years or so and dropped in on *his* childhood?

"I know it will work, Frank. It just needs someone who knows how to ride a sled!" the older boy named Edgar replies.

Frank?! Frank?! That boy is your *father!!*

You are so amazed at what you are seeing that you slip in the snow and fall in front of the woodshed. "Hey, there's someone there!" Edgar yells.

"Who are you? Come over here!" Frank — your father — calls. You pick yourself up but stand frozen beside the woodshed. Should you tell them who you really are? Would they believe such an unlikely story?

If you choose to tell them who you really are and where you've come from, turn to PAGE 34.

If you think maybe you'd better make up a story they'd be more likely to believe and that wouldn't frighten them, turn to PAGE 43.

Your trip through time is more exciting than you can imagine. The capsule is flooded in light so bright you have to shut your eyes. At times you feel weightless, as if you're floating in a dream. The hum of the machine becomes a roar, then a whistle, then music, then a hum again.

Then all sound and motion stop. You summon all your courage to look out the doorway. You have landed in the midst of a busy city. Silver cars float silently through the air. Silver-haired people dressed in silver suits glide by on a silently moving sidewalk. A sign across from a silver-domed building reads: SPACEPORT. Several spaceships stand pointing toward the sky.

Go on to the next page.

You have definitely traveled into the future!

Still shaky from the trip, you climb out of the Time Raider. Immediately, a crowd of people dressed in silver begins to gather. "Look at the funny clothes!" someone says, laughing. Everyone laughs and points at you.

"This way! This way!" a young man in a silver jumpsuit calls to you. "The spaceship is about to leave! Quickly! Follow me to the spaceship! Hurry — don't stand there staring at me!"

The crowd gets larger. Everyone is staring at you. "Look, the hair isn't silver!" someone cries.

"This way! Into the spaceship!" the young man calls.

"But I just got here!" you protest.

Should you follow the young man into the spaceship and see what adventures await you on board? Or should you stay and learn more about the silvery city you have just landed in? This is your next big decision.

If you choose to go on board the spaceship, turn to PAGE 11.

If you choose to stay and explore the city of the future, turn to PAGE 12.

10   You slowly step out of the Time Raider and look around. The capsule has landed you on the edge of the forest. On one side, the tall trees block out the sun. On the other side, a ragged lawn, strewn with old newspapers, pieces of wood, and objects of all sizes and shapes, leads up to a large house. Timidly, you walk up to the house.

"Come in, come in," Uncle Edgar says, greeting you at the door. "I want to show you my greatest creation ever."

"That's what you said about your last creation," you say. "Remember, the underwater pop-up toaster for deep-sea divers who like a big breakfast?"

"Forget about that," Uncle Edgar says. He takes you into his lab and shows you his newest invention — a time machine. Eagerly, he pushes you into the capsule and climbs in after you. The two of you are set to travel through time. But Uncle Edgar discovers he has forgotten his glasses. He leaves to go find them. You depart without him. You go backward in time. The trip seems to take no more than a second. You find yourself on the edge of a tall forest.

This story goes on forever, repeating itself without change. And you are trapped inside it. It's one of those sad stories about time travel — one of those sad stories that has no

END

The crowd of city dwellers begins to tighten around you, and you're not sure they're friendly. You push your way past them and run after the young man who called to you. He is running toward the spaceport, and you follow close behind.

"Quick! Into this ship!" he cries. He helps you up the ramp and into the dark ship. There are no lights inside. You stumble and fall. "Watch out!" an angry voice cries.

"Shut up, you!" another angry voice yells.

"Be quiet, all of you!" a voice bellows from a nearby loudspeaker. "Congratulations, Alrang! You have collected a hearty group of slaves for the Emperor!"

Slaves! The people around you hiss and grumble. The voice on the loudspeaker continues: "Silence, slaves! Welcome aboard the Emperor's slave ship! Your training will begin right after take-off!"

"We'll see about that," an angry voice whispers to you in the darkness.

What a mess! Your hand reaches up to the green pendant your uncle gave you. Should you squeeze it and return to the Time Raider? Or should you take your chances on the slave ship and see what the person whispering to you has in mind?

If you squeeze the pendant, turn to PAGE 18.
If you decide to stay on board, turn to PAGE 14.

The young man runs off to the spaceport, but you stay behind.

"Who are you?" people in the crowd demand. "Why are you dressed so funny?"

You decide you'd better tell them the truth. "I am a time traveler," you explain. "I come from Earth of the past."

A tall woman wearing a silver star on a silver uniform steps forward. "But we don't allow time travelers here," she says menacingly. "It's against the law. Didn't you see the signs?"

She points to a silver road sign next to the entrance. It reads: NO TIME TRAVELERS.

The tall woman grabs you up off the ground by the neck and holds you up to the crowd. "Who wants this illegal time traveler?"

"I do!" an old man with a silver beard cries. "It will make a wonderful hood ornament for my antique car — once I melt it down!"

"Let me have it!" a young woman cries. "My kids need a pet!"

Your hand reaches for the green pendant your Uncle Edgar gave you. Should you squeeze it and return to the safety of the Time Raider? Or should you stay in this strange city of the future and see what adventures await you?

If you wish to squeeze the pendant and escape from the silvery crowd, turn to PAGE 15.

If you wish to take your chances and spend more time in this city of the future, turn to PAGE 20.

14

In the dim light of the spaceship, you can see that you are surrounded by grim-looking people of all ages. They are dressed in silver, but their clothing is soiled and torn and the silver has little shine.

"Why does the Emperor need slaves?" you ask the bedraggled old man next to you.

"To lay eggs," the man says with a frown. "He will put us in coops and wait for us to lay eggs for his pantry."

"But that's ridiculous," you say a bit too loudly. "People can't lay eggs!"

"Of course not," the old man says sharply. "The Emperor is mad, completely mad. And unluckily for us, he adores eggs!"

"Hey, wait a minute!" a man with a long, silver beard says, looking at you. "Who are you? Why are you dressed like that?"

All of the sad, tired eyes aboard the slave ship turn toward you. Should you tell them the truth, that you are a time traveler from the past? They may not believe such a story. Perhaps it would be better to make up an explanation they would believe.

How should you decide what *to tell them? If you haven't told any lies — even white lies — to anyone you know for the past week, turn to PAGE 19.*

If you did tell a little white lie or two to someone you know during the past week, turn to PAGE 16.

"Let me outta here!" you tell yourself. "I don't think I have much future here in the future!"

You squeeze the green pendant and shut your eyes tightly. When you open your eyes, you expect to be back in the Time Raider.

But Uncle Edgar's inventions are not always perfect. The tall woman wearing the silver star is still holding you up to the crowd. You squeeze the pendant again and again. But it doesn't work.

You cannot escape.

Turn to PAGE 20. Maybe if you make the right moves — and have just a little luck — you can get out of this jam on your own!

"Well, it's all very simple to explain," you say slowly to the other passengers as you stall for time. "You see — uh — I'm just a humble vacuum cleaner salesperson, and my company thought it would be an attention-getter if I dressed this way. But then I got tricked into coming on board and —"

"What's a vacuum cleaner?" asks the old man.

"What's a company?" a woman with scraggly, silver hair asks.

"You're a liar!" another voice shouts.

"Liar!"

"Well, actually, I repair spaceships, you see. And I was doing some repairs on this one when it took off. So I really don't belong here —"

Go on to the next page.

Your story is interrupted by the cries of the other slaves.

"Spy! Spy! Spy!"

"You're a spy for the Emperor!" the old man yells, pointing a finger at you. Several slaves pounce on you and pin you to the floor.

Suddenly a soldier with blue skin, wearing a blue uniform to match, bursts into the slave quarters. The slaves back off and scatter. "Come with me," the blue soldier says, picking you off the floor with one giant hand. "The Emperor wants to see you. He has taken an interest in you."

He takes you to a walkway on the upper deck. A large, blue-faced man in a long, blue cape is looking down over the railing. It is the Emperor. As you approach, you realize that with one fast shove, you can push the Emperor over the railing to his death.

If you choose to kill the evil Emperor, turn to PAGE 27.

If you think it would be interesting to talk to your foe first and take your chances against him later, turn to PAGE 28.

18

Like all of Uncle Edgar's inventions, this one does not work perfectly all the time. You squeeze the green pendant again and again, but nothing happens.

You are stuck on board the slave ship. Go back to PAGE 14. Chin up. Things couldn't get worse — could they?!?

Honesty is the best policy, you decide. "I come from Earth of the past," you tell your fellow slaves. "I traveled through time and landed near the spaceport. Then I was tricked into entering this slave ship."

Do they believe your story? "We've heard of such things," the old man says. "Welcome to the year 3,000."

"You have come to lead our revolt against the Emperor and his men!" a woman calls from the corner.

"Who, me?" you say eloquently.

"Yes, you shall lead us!" the old man cries. He pulls out a small, silver gun. "A deathbeam gun," he says, shoving it into your hand. "Use it well."

"*What's going on in here?!*" a booming voice cries. A gigantic soldier with a bright blue face, dressed in a uniform to match, bursts into the slave quarters. He is obviously one of the Emperor's men. "*You, over there! What's that in your hand? Are you looking for a fight?*"

The giant soldier approaches. Should you back away? Try to explain your way out of this jam? Avoid a fight until everyone is organized and prepared to revolt? Or do you face the blue soldier and fight it out now?

If you decide to avoid a fight now, turn to PAGE 24.

If you decide to fight it out with the blue soldier, turn to PAGE 22.

"I can use the arms! Just the arms!" a little boy dressed in a silver jumpsuit yells.

"Yes! Tear the creature apart! Share it!" a woman's voice cries from the excited crowd.

"Put it down!" a loud voice cries suddenly. The woman drops you onto the ground with a *thud*. When you pick yourself up, you look up into the face of a man dressed all in gold!

"Crown Prince Randolph!" he addresses you. "You have arrived early! Your duel isn't until eighteen o'clock."

"Wha —?" you ask.

"Allow me to apologize for this crowd," the man in gold says, ushering you away. "They were just having some good-natured fun. Where is your spacecraft? I will escort you to the Duke's dueling chamber at once, your excellency."

The disappointed crowd watches as you exit with this man in gold. Have you traded one dilemma for another? Should you tell this man the truth — that you aren't Crown Prince Randolph and that you don't want to fight a duel? Or should you play along for a while to get safely away from the crowd? It's your decision.

If you decide to tell the man the truth, turn to PAGE 37.

If you think it smarter to play along for a while, turn to PAGE 40.

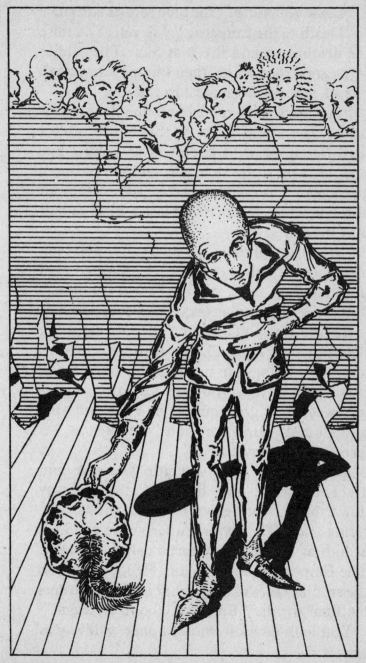

"Come here, slave!" the blue soldier screams.

"Death to the Emperor!" you yell. You raise the deathbeam and fire it at him. The soldier turns gray, then white, then slumps into a small pile of ash on the spaceship floor.

Four more soldiers rush into the slave chamber. Slaves jump them as they enter, and a hard-fought brawl is underway. A soldier hits the old man in the stomach, and the old man goes down. Outraged, you raise the deathbeam gun and, once again, you blast a blue soldier into ash.

"Stop the fighting!" a voice calls. You look to the upper walkway to see a blue-faced man in a long, blue robe. It is the Emperor himself! "Stop the fighting at once!" he commands.

But the slaves ignore him. They are defeating the Emperor's men. The Emperor sees that his forces are losing. He turns to flee back to the control room, but you leap up to the upper walkway. You grab him as he runs and spin him around. "How dare you!" he screams, his face turning purple.

Mustering all your strength, you give him a shove and he goes flying off the walkway down to the floor below. He lands with a shattering *thud!* The slaves gather around to look at him as his blue face turns paler and paler. The Emperor is about to die. He looks up into the smiling faces of the former slaves and utters his final words: "But what about my eggs?"

You look down from the upper walkway as

a happy cheer goes up. "You have rescued us, time traveler!" the old man yells.

You give them a final, triumphant smile, then reach for the green pendant. You will make an exit they'll never forget. You squeeze the green pendant and disappear from the slave ship. Breathing a sigh of relief, you find yourself back safe and sound in the Time Raider.

If you wish to travel even farther into the future, push the button marked FORWARD in the Time Raider and turn to PAGE 30.

If you'd prefer to go back to Uncle Edgar's house and see what he's up to in the present, push the button marked BACKWARD and turn to PAGE 32.

"Well, you see, sir, I was thirsty," you say hesitantly to the soldier. You try to hide the deathbeam gun under your shirt cuff. "I thought maybe if I asked politely, you might give me a —"

The blue soldier picks you up roughly by the neck and carries you over to a table. "What a bore," he mutters. "I always have to make an example of someone on every trip."

He turns a switch, and a blue light beams down on you. He holds you under the blue light, and you begin to feel funny. You feel as if you're shrinking. You look down at your body, and you seem to be growing feathers. You try to peck at the blue soldier with your beak, but he's holding you away from him. *"Cluck cluck cluck,"* you tell him.

He turns off the blue light. You flap your wings and scratch at the table. The blue soldier tosses some gravel onto the table, and you gobble it up in your beak.

"Good heavens," you tell yourself — your last human thought — "the Emperor is going to get his eggs after all!"

THE END

You feel yourself spinning and tumbling back through time. The Time Raider lands with a bounce and a jolt, and when your head stops bouncing and jolting, you look out on a clearing at the edge of another wooded area. Have you landed at the same forest?

No. In the clearing are two log cabins. Some men are putting a log roof on a third cabin. From their dress, you figure that you have landed on the frontier in early American pioneer days. But you don't have long to think about where you are.

As you climb out of the Time Raider, you see that you have landed next to a large, primitively built barn. And the barn is on fire!

"Fire! Fire!" the men working on the roof are screaming. About a dozen horses come running out of the barn. "The barn is on fire!" The cry goes up through the small settlement.

"There's the person who started the fire!" a woman screams, pointing at you from the doorway of a cabin. "The stranger there — the stranger set the barn on fire!"

The men are down off the roof now and are chasing after you with fury in their eyes. Do you run from them? Or do you stay and face them and tell them the truth?

If you choose to run, turn to PAGE 60.

If you choose to stay and talk to them, turn to PAGE 36.

"Die, evil one!" you scream as you shove the Emperor over the railing with all your might.

All your might, however, is not worth much. No one told you about the Emperor's gravity-shoes, which keep him solidly and safely rooted to the floor.

He chuckles and holds a small ray gun up to your face. *ZZZZZAPPP.*

A few seconds later, you are a small, lacquered figure on his coffee table. You're quite a conversation piece when company comes to visit. No one can figure out what that embroidered word on your back pocket means — *Levi's.*

THE END

"Here is the lowly slave you requested, Emperor," the blue soldier says, shoving you toward the Emperor.

The Emperor gives you a broad smile with his bright blue lips. "You are not like the others," he says quietly, eyeing you closely. "From whence do you come?"

"From Earth of the past," you explain, your voice quivering a little in the face of such power. "I am a time traveler. I'm here by accident, actually."

"I thought as much," the Emperor says thoughtfully. "Do you lay eggs?"

"No, sir."

The Emperor does not believe you. "You *must* lay eggs for me," he says. "I will not take no for an answer."

He does not return you to the other slaves. He keeps you in his private chamber and makes you tell him all about Earth of the past. When you reach his home planet, he allows you to walk with him in his castle garden. He is very curious about the past. He wants to know everything.

As you walk, he bursts into tears. "I have no eggs," he says. "The slaves produce no eggs at all. Surely, I will perish!" He kicks a chicken out of the way.

"Hey, wait a minute!" you cry. "That's a chicken!"

"So what?" he says irritably.

"What do you use chickens for on your planet?"

"For kicking," he answers. "They're great for kicking." He kicks another chicken that dares to cross his path.

"But chickens lay eggs," you inform him.

Those three words make you a national hero.

The slaves are all freed. Chickens take their places in the coops. The happy Emperor proclaims every day a holiday. And there are free eggs for everyone!

If you wish to travel even farther into the future, squeeze the green pendant, return to your time machine, and turn to PAGE 30.

If you'd prefer to go back to Uncle Edgar's house and see what he's up to in the present, squeeze the green pendant, return to the Time Raider, and turn to PAGE 32.

If you would like a break after your heroic triumph, close the book. You've earned a rest!

THE END

The Time Raider bobs and bounces its way into the future. Orbs of light grow from tiny, white specks, engulf the capsule, then fade before your eyes. Your ears are filled with eerie melodies no human ears have ever heard.

You land softly, in silence. It is the loudest silence you can imagine, a white silence that makes you hesitate before pushing open the door to the Time Raider. You look out into a crowded city of the future.

It is city of low, almost flat buildings. The streets and walkways are filled with people who look just like humans of our day — except for one big difference.

No one is moving.

Everyone is frozen to the spot on which he or she stands. The people of this city seem calm in their stillness. They do not seem to be uncomfortable or in pain. They just are not moving.

You look from face to face as you run through the still, silent streets. You look for a blink of an eye, a quick smile, the twitch of a finger. There is no movement. You reach out and grab a man's hand. It is warm to the touch.

Can these unmoving people be *alive?*

You walk for blocks through this strange city, looking for the bobbing head of a pigeon, even a crawling insect — but nothing moves.

"Perhaps these people have been frozen like this by someone who wishes to control time," you tell yourself. "Or perhaps they have some sort of illness. Should I try to get them moving again? Should I try to help them?"

Then you remind yourself that you have traveled to the future not to interfere, but to explore. "Maybe it's none of my business what has happened here," you tell yourself. "Maybe I'd be causing a lot of trouble by trying to help."

It's your decision now.

If you decide to help the frozen citizens of this silent city, turn to PAGE 38.

If you decide just to explore the planet, turn to PAGE 46.

"You didn't wait for me," Uncle Edgar says, pouting. "How could you leave without me? After all, the Time Raider is *my* invention!"

Your apologies don't seem to change his mood. He is heartbroken that he didn't have a chance to travel through time.

"Okay," you finally say, "why don't we take the Time Raider out for another trip?" You are exhausted and every bone in your body aches. But you know that Uncle Edgar won't stop complaining until he gets to travel in his marvelous machine.

"What an excellent suggestion," Uncle Edgar says, brightening immediately, smiling his first smile since your return. "Let's go!"

He pushes you into the capsule and climbs in after you. He begins turning dials and pushing buttons, and soon the machine sputters and then hums.

"Now, did you remember your glasses this time?" you ask.

"Yes, I've got my glasses," he says, scowling at you. "What do you think I am — forgetful?"

"No comment," you say, chuckling. "Did you bring a jacket in case we land in cold weather?"

"Gee, no, I didn't," Uncle Edgar says. "I'd better go get one."

He pushes open the door to the capsule and climbs out. You have a good laugh at his expense.

But your laugh doesn't last long. The time machine begins to whistle and shake. It's about to leave, and Uncle Edgar is going to miss it again! Can you stop it?

There are three buttons. One of them will stop the machine. Quick! You must press one of them!

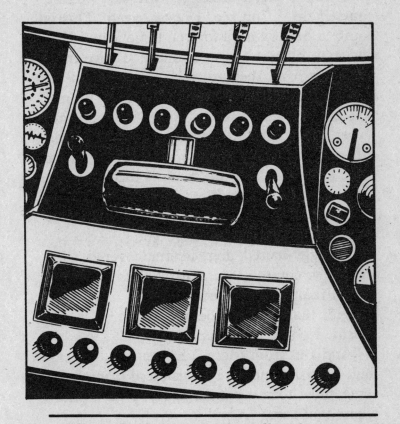

If you decide to press the yellow button, turn to PAGE 39.

If you decide to press the blue button, turn to PAGE 57.

If you decide to press the white button, turn to PAGE 90.

"Well, I — uh — you see —" you stammer, slipping again in the snow and making a three-point landing on your hands and nose.

"Why were you hiding behind the shed?" your father asks.

"I wasn't exactly hiding," you say, pulling yourself up. "You see, I just arrived. This is going to be very hard for you to believe." You decide to blurt it all out at once. "I have traveled here from the future. I traveled back in time about forty years." You turn to Frank, who is staring at you, smirking. "You are my father," you tell him. "And you are my Uncle Edgar. At least you will be several years from now. And you'll invent the time machine that brings me back here."

There is silence for a while. Everyone stares at everyone. Do they believe you?

A shaggy-haired dog, its fur covered with wet snow, comes running up. "This is my sister," Frank says, petting the dog. "And that squirrel that just ran behind that tree is my cousin. I come from Jupiter."

"And I'm from Mars," Edgar says, chuckling. "I just came here to visit and bring back some snow to my planet. Do you have snow where you came from?"

"Of *course*," you say, hurt that they don't believe you. "You see, I —"

"Do they have snow like this?" Frank asks. He dumps a huge armload of snow over your head. It drips under your collar and down your back. You don't even have time to shiver before both of them dump another load of snow on top of you.

Angrily, you shove them away. They shove you back. Before you realize it, you are rolling around in the snow, punching and kicking at your father and uncle. You take a hard punch in the stomach, and you realize your lip is bleeding.

"Hey, I don't need this!" you tell yourself. You leap up and begin running toward the Time Raider. You can hear the cries of "Chicken! Chicken!" and raucous laughter behind you, but you don't care. Who wants to get beat up by your own father?

You slip and stumble your way to the Time Raider. Out of breath, your cut lip bleeding onto the snow, you pry open the door and jump inside.

Now, how to get back to Uncle Edgar's lab? You reach for the button marked FORWARD. Do you push it once? Or twice? You're not sure. You'll just have to take a chance.

If you decide to push it once, turn to PAGE 58.

If you decide to push it twice, turn to PAGE 53.

"The stranger started the fire!" someone yells.

"Wait a minute. Hold everything!" you cry as they run toward you. "I can explain!"

"Cut! Stop everything!" an angry voice yells from the opposite side of the clearing.

An angry man in modern dress, carrying a clipboard, comes running up to you. Everyone else comes to a complete halt. "How did this kid get on the set?" the man screams angrily. He turns to you. "You've ruined the whole scene! We've got to rebuild the barn and burn it all over again! Half a million dollars lost and at least a day's shooting! And I promised the studio I'd bring in *Son of Daniel Boone, Kung Fu Master* under budget!"

Uncle Edgar has done it again. His invention didn't carry you back in time; it merely carried you to a movie on location in California. You apologize to the frantic movie director and ask if there's anything you can do to make up for the damage you've done.

"Well . . . as a matter of fact, there is," he says slyly. "How would you like to be in the movies?" He gives you a job as a stuntperson. Your stunt is to fall off a horse into a mud-filled watering trough. After thirty-four tries, you do it correctly.

Your efforts will later end up on the cutting room floor. But you don't care. You're just glad this story has come to

THE END

"Just a moment," you say. "There's something I think I should tell you." The man in gold drops your arm and stares at you as you explain. "I'm not Crown Prince Randolph. I'm a time traveler from Earth of the past. I landed here a few moments ago and —"

"Oh. Sorry. My mistake," the man says, looking embarrassed. He picks you up by the neck and carries you back to the woman with the silver star. "Here's your illegal," he tells her. "It's not the Crown Prince after all."

The woman hands you to the old man with the silver beard, who was the first to ask for you. He takes you home, melts you down until you are two inches tall, coats you in silver, and then attaches you to the hood of his 1948 Packard sedan.

Believe it or not, you make a very nice-looking hood ornament. And sitting on the front of the car like that, you'll get to see a lot of this world of the future. That is, if the old man ever finds an engine so that he can take the ancient car out of its garage!

THE END

"I must help these people!" you say to yourself. "There must be something wrong here, or they wouldn't be standing all over the city, as if unaware that anything happened to them."

You run from one block to another. You don't know what to look for, or even where to look. "Perhaps the answer is inside one of these low buildings," you tell yourself. You try to decide which building to enter.

You do not see the hidden camera that has been following you since you arrived. You do not know that the camera is sending your picture back to a scientific lab hidden under the street upon which you stand.

Inside the lab, a tall, bearded scientist named Dr. Chandon is viewing your every move with alarm. He calls his assistant over to him and says, "Something has activated one of the robots. All of the robots in this model city are supposed to be switched off. But look on the viewscreen, Almador. One of them is moving!"

The two men stand watching you on their viewscreen. A few seconds later, they are up on the street, coming toward you with six of their armed guards.

If you think maybe you'd better make a run for it, turn to PAGE 56.

If you think you'd rather explain to Dr. Chandon exactly who you are, turn to PAGE 66.

Way to go!
You pressed the cigarette lighter.
That won't be much help to you, especially since you don't smoke.

Why don't you go back to PAGE 33 and press another button?

"Call me Arnule," the man in gold tells you. "I am First Regent to the Duke. I believe you will find the Duke a worthy opponent. He fights five duels a day. He is a fabulous sportsman. He has killed four people already this morning!"

"Great," you mutter. Your knees begin to shake. Your eyes blur. You don't even see the magnificent artificial rainbow or the transparent, domed office buildings you are passing on your way to the Duke's palace.

"The Duke loves sports," Arnule tells you. "But killing people makes him sad. What a pity that someone must die in every game."

"Yes, it's a pity," you hear yourself repeat. "Why doesn't the Duke take up chess or badminton then?"

"What's *that?*" Arnule asks, looking at you suspiciously.

But you have no time to answer. The Duke himself greets you at the entrance to his dueling chamber. He is a short, young man with wavy, blond hair and friendly, blue eyes. "I've looked forward to our game," he says, shaking your hand. He leads you into the brightly lit hall where your duel is to take place.

"Uh — there's something I should tell you," you say, your voice shaking.

"There is nothing you need say," the Duke says. "Your ability with the antique sword is known across this galaxy. But I have been practicing, Randolph. I think I will give you a good game." He picks up a sword. "Arnule, come here at once!" he calls angrily. "This sword — it still has blood on it from my last duel! Have it cleaned immediately."

Arnule takes the sword and rushes out of the chamber with it. This gives you a few brief seconds to plan a strategy. You squeeze the green pendant to get you out of this mess, but it doesn't work.

If you pick up a sword and fight him, chances are you won't survive long enough to congratulate him on his swordsmanship. But maybe — just maybe — you will get off with a slight wound and then you can explain who you really are.

If only you could think of a way to stall him, a way to get his attention on some other subject. But you can't think of anything at all, and Arnule is returning with the now spotless sword!

What do you choose to do?

If you feel you have no choice but to go ahead with this duel and hope for a lucky break, pick a number from one to ten. Remember your number, and turn to PAGE 48. Good luck!

If you'd like to try to stall and hope against hope that you'll come up with a bright idea to save your life, turn to PAGE 50.

"Well — I — uh — you see," you stammer eloquently.

The two boys forget about their sled and walk over to you, their big boots crunching in the snow. "We haven't seen you around before," your father says to you, acting tough.

"I just moved here," you say. (So far, you haven't told a lie!) "I — uh — was admiring your sled. I don't have one."

"We don't have one, either," your father grumbles. "Thanks to the boy inventor here."

"You're wrong! You're wrong!" Uncle Edgar starts to whine. You force yourself to keep from laughing, but it sure strikes you funny seeing your old uncle as a red-faced boy about to throw a tantrum.

The two boys are still eyeing you suspiciously. "Why don't we try it out?" you ask, trying desperately to keep them from asking questions about you. "Maybe it just needs to be broken in."

"Yeah, come on, Frank — the kid's right," Edgar says eagerly.

The three of you climb the snowy hill, with Edgar pulling the sled behind him. Suddenly a woman's voice floats through the frozen air. "Edgar, Frank — come in now! I've got hot apple pie for you!"

You turn back and see a young woman in the doorway of the house. It's your grandmother! "Hey, don't stop, kid," Edgar says, pulling at your coat. "First the sled."

Your grandmother, waving and calling from

the back door, becomes smaller and smaller as the three of you climb the hill.

Finally you reach the top. Looking down, you see for the first time that there is a frozen lake on the other side. "All we need is a little more weight on the sled," Edgar says seriously. Frank doesn't agree, but he reluctantly climbs on. Edgar climbs on top of him. "Give us a push, kid," Frank tells you. "If this works, you can have the next ride."

You give the sled a push with all your strength. It starts slowly at first, then picks up speed and, despite the weight on it, heads toward the lake.

And then tragedy interrupts this beautiful wintry scene of the past.

The sled bumps onto the lake and the air is filled with the sound of cracking ice. The ice breaks apart, the sled tips, then topples. Frank and Edgar start to scream, but their scream capsizes with them. In seconds, as you stare in horror, they spill into the icy waters, the sled bobbing and splashing on top of them.

No one else is in view. Only you can save their lives. You run, stumbling and falling, down the steep hill, your heart pounding. Can you get there in time to pull them out?

Go on to the next page.

Run! Run as fast as you can, but it's all a matter of luck. Will you be lucky or unlucky? Pick a number between one and ten.

If you chose one, two, or three, turn to PAGE 47.

If you chose four, five, or six, turn to PAGE 52.

If you chose seven, eight, nine, or ten, turn to PAGE 54.

Good luck!!

"I mustn't let my imagination run away with me," you tell yourself. "If these people are frozen here, there must be a good reason. I'll just take a walk through this amazing city and see what clues I can pick up about —"

Suddenly you stop. You realize that these people aren't frozen as you thought. Everyone is moving — moving very slowly.

"These people seem to live at a different speed than I do," you say. "But they are definitely moving, just much slower than people of my day. Perhaps the gravity of Earth has changed, and the people have adapted to it by living at a slower pace."

Slowly, a young woman walks toward you. You stare at her, waiting for her to reach you. "Whooooo aaaaaaaare yooooooooou?" she asks in a deep voice that sounds like a record played too slowly. "Yooooooou muuuuuust hellllllllllp uuuuuuuuuus."

Slowly a crowd of people gathers around you. You listen patiently as the woman, one slow syllable at a time, explains that a tyrant from another planet has taken over the city. She begs you to rescue them.

"What can I do?" you say. "I'm not even functioning at the right speed. How can I help?"

If you decide to try to help them anyway, turn to PAGE 68.

If you decide you must refuse to help, turn to PAGE 81.

Bad news.

You fell into a deep snowdrift and didn't get there in time. Edgar and Frank were both lost.

This means that you were never born.

You'd better put down this book. It is meant to be read only by people who were born!

THE END

48

Here's how your duel with the Duke came out:

If the number you picked was one or two:
You accidentally skewered yourself before the Duke had a chance to pick up his sword. It was the shortest duel in history, and you became a national laughingstock. From that day on, whenever anyone in the kingdom did anything exceptionally clumsy, they said they had "pulled a Prince Randolph."

THE END

If the number you picked was three, four, or five:
Better you shouldn't know what happened to you! Yecccch! Close the book and try to forget you were ever here.

THE END

Go on the the next page.

If the number you picked was six, seven, or eight:

You put up a tremendous battle, but the Duke quickly overpowered you with his lightning-fast sword moves and fancy footwork. After a few minutes of swordplay, he moved in for the kill. But his sword pierced the green pendant around your neck, and you found yourself magically transported, safe and sound, back to the Time Raider. Whew! What a close one! For further instructions, turn to PAGE 30.

If the number you picked was nine or ten:

A miracle! You've defeated the Duke. Congratulations — you're the new dueling champion! But before you start to celebrate, better take a look at who's waiting outside the dueling chamber. Every sportsman and sportswoman in the kingdom wants to challenge the new champion. You're going to have your hands full for quite a while. Good luck — and don't forget to yell *touché!*

THE END

The Duke hands you a sword, and you stand facing each other for a moment. "I am sorry you must die. Truly sorry," the Duke says. "But a game is a game."

His words give you an idea. "Just a second," you say, putting down the sword. You reach into your pocket and find a pencil and a small piece of paper. "Let me show you something," you say, calling the Duke over to you.

You scribble furiously on the piece of paper as the Duke looks over your shoulder. "Lines? Squares? What is this foolishness?" he cries.

"It's a game," you say, marking an X in one of the squares you have drawn. "Now, you draw an O in one of the squares," you tell him. "Try to block me from getting three squares in a row."

"But — but, I don't understand!" cries the Duke, taking the pencil. "How can I kill you by making little O's and X's?"

You explain that no one dies in this game.

"A game in which no one dies?! You're a genius!" the Duke cries, writing another O in a square. "Why didn't *we* ever think of that!"

The game of "Randolph," in which nobody dies, sweeps the nation. The Duke thanks you by playing game after game with you until your fingers are red and raw, and the pencil is a tiny stub. Happy and victorious, you bid him farewell and return through the silver streets to your time machine.

Go on to the next page.

The Time Raider never looked better! You find yourself whistling "Home, Sweet Home"! But what is your next move?

If you'd like to take a break, close the book and try to forget about the color silver for a while.

THE END

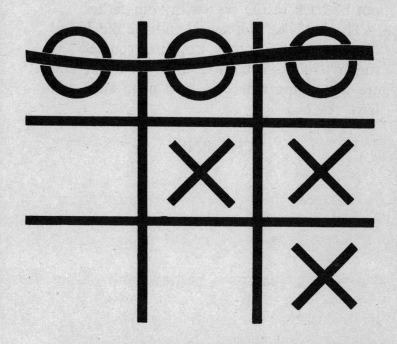

If you'd like to travel farther into the future for more adventures, push the button in the Time Raider marked FORWARD, and turn to PAGE 30.

If you'd rather go back to the present and find out what Uncle Edgar is doing back in his lab, push the button marked BACKWARD, and turn to PAGE 32.

52 Good news and bad news.

Heroically you managed to pull your father out of the freezing waters, but your Uncle Edgar was lost.

As you help your father back to the house, you realize that Uncle Edgar did not live to build his time machine. This means that you cannot travel in time. This means that you cannot be back in the past with your father.

The icy lake, the snow, and the old house disappear immediately. You find yourself sitting in a room. You are reading this book. You are wondering where to turn next since you have reached

THE END

You push the button twice. A few seconds later, you find yourself, still cold and wet, back in Uncle Edgar's lab. "Well? What happened? Anything exciting?" he asks, eagerly pulling you out of the capsule.

"I went back in time," you tell him. "I saw you and Dad when you were boys. You couldn't get your sled to work. You dumped snow on me. We had a fight. I tried to tell you who I was, but you didn't believe me."

Uncle Edgar has a broad smile on his face and his eyes seem far away. "I remember it," he says. "I do! I remember it well! Frank and I were arguing over my new rudder. Some strange kid interrupted us. . . ."

"That was me!" you cry excitedly.

"Imagine!" Uncle Edgar says, still off in a faraway memory. "It was you! What a small world!"

"That's all you have to say?" you cry. "What a small world? That's it?"

"One other thing," Uncle Edgar says. You eagerly await his words. "Chicken! Chicken! Why didn't you stay and fight?"

Even time travelers don't get much respect these days!

THE END

Your feet slip in the wet snow, and you fall forward into a deep drift. The sled still bobs in the water. One of the boys lifts an arm up, attempts to grab the sled, and fails.

You've *got* to get there!

You're half-running, half-crawling now. "I'm coming!" you scream in a wild voice you don't recognize. "I'm coming!"

You reach the end of the lake. You crawl out onto the crackling, crumbling ice. You reach — reach — as far as your arm will reach, crawling slowly farther and farther toward the break in the ice.

You've got an arm!

You pull. It's your father! Pull! He is spluttering and shaking. He scrambles up onto the firm ice. Safe! Now Uncle Edgar. Back you reach. You grab the waiting hand. Pull! Now Uncle Edgar is up. Now he is safe.

But you must get them to the house before frostbite sets in. Can they walk? Yes. You pull them and push them. You must get them to the house! You *must!*

It seems like hours later, but it is only a few minutes when you open the back door, and the three of you stagger into the warm, fragrant kitchen. Now it all seems like a blur of feverish activity to you.

Your grandmother, a terrified young woman at first, overcomes her fright, swings into action, and gets the boys changed, warms them up by the fire, and doesn't even take time to ask who you are or where you came from.

Later, the hot cocoa and apple pie. You know you'll never forget the taste, the feel of the fire on your frozen face, the warm glow of the fireplace, the soft words of the woman who many years later will be your grandmother.

"You saved my sons' lives," she says quietly, calm now after her terror and fevered activity. "I don't even know your name."

Should you tell them the truth? Your father and Uncle Edgar, still shaken, still trying to warm their bones, stare at you now, as if seeing you for the first time. It seems like the right time to tell them. You *must* let them know who you are! "I come from far away," you begin softly. "You probably won't believe this, but—"

"Before you tell us, have another piece of pie," your grandmother says. As she hands you the plate, she accidentally bumps the green pendant around your neck.

You find yourself back in the Time Raider, hurtling forward in time, toward the present and Uncle Edgar's lab. Your story went untold. But it's just as well.

They wouldn't have believed you anyway!

THE END

"Stop that robot!" the tall, bearded man yells. The armed guards rush forward.

You don't like the look of things, so you turn and run. Why did that man call you a robot?

You run through the crowded streets, bumping into the silent, frozen citizens of this strange city. The guards are right behind you. The tall, bearded man is yelling, "Robot malfunction! Robot malfunction!" as he and the other man run behind the guards.

As you run, you begin to realize why they are so excited. This is a city of robots — and they believe you are one of them! You are running as fast as you can. You trip over an old man and knock him over. He lies frozen where he falls, his eyes staring straight ahead.

Suddenly you run into a wall. There is nowhere to run. You seem to have come to the end of this city. The guards are closing in. You see a control panel of some sort. What appears to be a master switch sticks out of the wall. Your hand reaches up to it even though you don't know what it controls or what it might do.

If you decide to pull the switch, turn to PAGE 62.

If you decide you'd rather play it safe and squeeze the green pendant around your neck to get you out of this situation, turn to PAGE 78.

You did it!

The blue button stopped the machine.

Here comes Uncle Edgar now, carrying his jacket. "Okay, let's get going," he says. "I can't wait!"

You notice, however, that he is no longer wearing his glasses. "Where are they?" you ask.

"Oh, my goodness," he says. "I must be getting a little forgetful. I took them off and put them down so that I could see in my closet better. I'll go get them. Back in a jiffy."

Once again he climbs out of the time capsule.

And once again the machine starts humming and bouncing. You are just about out of patience with your uncle. "It would serve him right if I took off again without him," you say, and the idea gives you a good laugh. "But could I really do that to Uncle Edgar?"

If you'd prefer to leave without him, sit back, press the red button, and turn to PAGE 82.

If you have the patience to wait for him, press the blue button twice and turn to PAGE 87.

You push the button once, close your eyes, take a deep breath, and realize that nothing is happening. You push the button again. Nothing.

"Hey, come out of there!" Frank is calling. "Come out and fight, Chicken!"

Edgar begins pounding on the roof of the Time Raider. "We'll tear this sled apart!" he yells.

"No! Stop!" you cry, shoving open the door and climbing out. "This isn't a sled, it's a time machine!"

"Sure!" cries Frank. "And this isn't snow! It's magical fairy dust from the moon!"

"Let's tear this thing apart, Frank, and teach this kid not to tell fibs!" Uncle Edgar cries.

You cannot do anything to stop them. Who would believe it? Before your very eyes, Uncle Edgar is ripping apart his own time machine.

They have a great time pulling the Time Raider to shreds. When they have completely demolished it, they turn to where you were sitting in the snow. "Now, who are you *really?*" Frank starts to ask.

But you have vanished.

"Where'd the kid go?" Edgar asks.

They don't know.

And we don't know, either.

Perhaps the Uncle Edgar of the future could explain what happened to you.

But right now, he's just a twelve-year-old boy, heading home with his brother for a slice of hot apple pie and a cup of cocoa.

We hope you find yourself before this book
goes on much further. We'll all miss you!

THE END

The flames pour out of the barn as you turn and run toward the woods. The angry cries of the settlers are right behind you. You don't turn back to see how close they are. You just run straight ahead as fast as you can.

The roar of the fire becomes a whisper as you duck into the thick woods and zigzag through the trees. The voices still follow, but they are farther back. Can you lose them? What will they do to you if they catch you?

These questions flash through your mind as you dodge and twist through the trees. Then up ahead you see a large, hollowed-out oak tree. You dash inside it and hold your breath as the settlers run right past you. Phew! Safe for a while.

Later, you come out from the tree and, at a slower pace, you pick your way through the woods in the opposite direction. The only sounds you hear now are forest sounds — and the crunch of your own footsteps. Suddenly, you are in a small clearing. There, less than twenty yards from you, you see a boy about your age. He is dressed in buckskin and carries a long hunting rifle. And he is running in terror from a gigantic brown bear!

If you think you'd better stop and help him escape from the bear, turn to PAGE 64.

If you think you'd be smarter to keep fleeing from the settlers and avoid the bear, turn to PAGE 67.

Your hand grasps the switch tightly, and you pull down with all your strength. You don't have to wait long to see the results.

Immediately, all the people of the town come to life. They begin stretching their arms and legs, looking around, and talking. "Someone has rescued us," a young man says.

"Where is Dr. Chandon?" a woman asks.

You are so startled to see everyone come to life that you do not notice what has happened to the armed guards and the two men who commanded them. As a crowd of people begins to gather around you, you see that the guards and the two men are frozen now, unmoving and silent.

"What have I done?" you ask yourself as the people you have freed form a circle around you. They are staring at you now and asking so many questions all at once you cannot make out the words. "Have I freed these robots and frozen the people who built them? Have I accidently turned things upside down here and allowed the wrong side to triumph?"

A young man steps forward from the crowd and soon sets your mind at ease. "We want to thank you for rescuing us," he says, shaking your hand. "You have freed us from the slavery of our robot-masters."

"What do you mean?" you ask, totally confused. "Are you all robots?"

This gets a big laugh from the crowd. "We are not robots," the young man says. "We are humans. The men you have stopped — Dr.

Chandon, his assistant, and the guards — are robots. They are robots we created to be our leaders."

You are stunned by this news. "You mean you built robots to lead you?"

"Yes," the young man continues. "We knew that humans are imperfect, and we wanted perfect leaders. So we built robots to lead us. But we didn't know that our robot-masters would begin to treat *us* like robots. And that they'd find a way to control our every move. Dr. Chandon, our master-robot, kept us frozen until he had tasks for us. But you have defeated him."

"Well, I hope in the future you will remember what happened and will elect humans to be your leaders," you say.

This gets a very big laugh from the crowd. "*Humans* to be leaders? You have a very good sense of humor!" the young man says, and the crowd laughs again for a long while.

"We just have to build better robots in the future," the young man says. "I'm sure we can do it. After all, humans can do anything! Right?"

"Right," you say as you squeeze the green pendant around your neck, eager to escape from this crazy future world!

THE END

"Hellllp! Ohhh — hellllp!" the boy screams. He has good reason to scream. The bear is right on his heels. A giant, brown paw swipes at the boy's back. The bear growls its pleasure in the pursuit.

"Your rifle!" you scream to the boy, running as fast as you can toward him. "Throw me your rifle!" You've never held a rifle in your life, but it seems like a sensible thing to try.

The boy tosses you the hunting rifle and keeps running. You follow, running at top speed. You raise the rifle to your shoulder, stop, aim at the sky, and pull the trigger. The gun roars in response and thrusts you back to the ground.

You look up, surrounded by gunsmoke. The rifle shot has frightened the bear. It turns and runs off into the woods. The terrified boy grabs onto a tree trunk, and grasps it, breathing heavily, gasping and shaking, trying to regain control.

You walk over slowly, listening for the cries and footsteps of the settlers, who must have heard the rifle shot. "That was a close one," you say quietly.

The boy is still shaking all over. "You saved mah life," he manages to get out with much effort. "Allow me to introduce mahself, stranger. The name is Dan'l Boone."

The great trailblazer Daniel Boone? Shaking and crying because he was chased by a bear?

You hand him back his rifle. "Why didn't you use this?" you ask.

"I'm a-scared of guns," he says, a chill running down his back. "I think I'm more scared o' guns than I am o' b'ars." He wipes a tear from his eye.

"Oh, you'll get over it. I'm sure of it," you say soothingly. You think you might tell him of the courage he will show later in life. But your thoughts are interrupted by the cry of a settler — from very close by.

"There's the stranger! We've got the varmint now! Look out! The stranger has pulled a gun on young Dan'l! Drop that rifle, stranger! You've already got barn-burnin' on your conscience. Don't add a murder!"

The settlers are closing in on you. Do you try to explain? Or is running away from them a wiser move?

If you choose to stay and explain, turn to PAGE 92.

If you choose to keep running and try to escape, turn to PAGE 72.

The guards form a circle around you as Dr. Chandon and his assistant approach. "Hello," you say, trying to sound friendly. "It's nice to see someone *moving* around here!"

Dr. Chandon doesn't answer. "A malfunction in the nerve-to-brain mechanism," he says to his assistant. "Don't bother trying to repair it. Just replace the whole circuitry."

"Allow me to introduce myself," you say, still trying to make some contact with the unfriendly scientist. Once again, your effort is ignored. "I have come from far away," you say.

"It's babbling out random sentences," Dr. Chandon says, a little surprised. "Grab it and change its brain-activity mode."

Your efforts to explain yourself sound like random babbling to these people. They grab you and go to work right there on the street. Within minutes, they have replaced your insides with a brand-new motor and your brain with the latest-model thought-capacitator.

Try not to feel sorry for yourself. Most likely, some fabulous adventures await you in your new identity as a robot. Just think good thoughts and keep those circuits clear!

THE END

You run through the clearing without slowing down — past the boy, past the bear chasing the boy. You feel bad about not helping out the boy. But you know you wouldn't get a chance to explain if the settlers caught up with you.

Unfortunately, you seem to have caught the bear's attention. He leaves the boy behind, turns toward the woods, and chases after you. For a bear, he's a very fast runner. He has almost caught up with you. The growls seem to get louder, but they're not; they're just getting closer!

You turn back to see how near the bear is, trip over an exposed tree root, and fall flat on your face on the damp, mossy ground.

Do you scramble away? Keep running until you can figure out a way to explain to the settlers that you didn't burn their barn? Or do you escape by pushing the green pendant around your neck and return to the Time Raider?

If you choose to push the pendant, turn to PAGE 73.

If you'd rather take your chances against the bear, turn to PAGE 71.

"Pleeeeeeeease. Yooooooooou musssssssssst helllllllllp," a young man steps forward and begs.

"Well, I don't know what —" Your words are interrupted by the sound of marching boots. An army of fierce-looking soldiers, dressed in shiny, black uniforms and carrying strange, triple-barreled guns, comes marching in slow motion into view. The army is led by a bloated, green creature with the face of a snail — obviously the tyrant from another planet.

As the triple-barreled guns are raised and pointed at you, you swing into action. You leap at the first soldier and knock him over easily. You are moving ten times faster than everyone else — a real advantage! Before they can fire a single shot, you have disarmed the entire army and taken the slow-moving snail creature as your prisoner!

"Yaaaaaaaaaaaaaaay! Threeeeeeeeeeee cheeeeeeeeeeeers!" the crowd roars, in deep, slow-moving unison.

You suddenly realize that because of your amazing speed, you are a superhero here. You can go anywhere, do anything, defeat anyone — in one-tenth the time of anyone else.

You decide to stay and become a legendary folk hero to these people. You wipe out crime because no criminal is fast enough to escape from you. You use your lightning speed to rescue people from disasters. You help build tall buildings in the time it normally took these people to dig the hole for the foundation.

Books are written about you (you are known

as "Young Lightning"). Movies are made about your speedy exploits. The life of a superhero is very gratifying to you.

The only time you regret your decision is when you are standing in line at the super-market, because it always moooooooooooooooooooooves liiiiiiiiiiiiiiiiiiiike thiiiiiiiiiiiiiiiiiiiiiiiiiiiiiiisssssssssssssssssssss!

THE END

The bear is about to wrap its paws around your neck, when a voice — the voice of the boy you ran past — cries out, "Stop, Otto! Stop playing with the stranger like that!"

Otto, the bear, backs away immediately and looks embarrassed. "Otto, I'm ashamed of you," the boy says, pointing a finger at the now forlorn bear.

"He — he understands you? He obeys?" you manage to stammer, still feeling the paws around your neck.

"Oh, yes, he understands very well," the boy says, patting the bear affectionately on the stomach. "He understands three languages, actually. He's a circus bear, you see. We were rehearsing our act when you —"

Something has distracted Otto. It is your green pendant. Before you can do anything to stop him, Otto has given the pendant a squeeze.

Otto disappears before your eyes. You are glad to know that he understands three languages. That will come in handy in his travels through time.

As for you, you decide on the spot to change your name to Davy Crockett. Perhaps it will bring you luck in your new life as an early American pioneer.

THE END

One of the settlers makes a grab for you, but you duck from his grasp and head for the woods. Can you escape them a second time? You doubt it. You used up most of your energy during your first run.

But the woods are thick, and you are short enough to get lost among the tangled shrubs and in the shadows of the trees. You run until you feel as though your lungs are going to give out.

Then you realize that the footsteps behind you are not being made by any settler. A furious brown bear is chasing you, an angry bear who doesn't like people who fire rifles at him.

The bear roars and lunges toward you. You feel its hot, wet breath on your neck.

Is it time to push the green pendant around your neck and return to the Time Raider? Or do you want to take your chances against the bear so that you can stay and clear your name with the settlers?

If it's stay-and-fight, turn to PAGE 74.
If it's push-and-run, turn to PAGE 77.

You reach up to squeeze the green pendant, but the bear swats it away with one swipe of a giant, brown paw. You have no choice now but to stay and fight it out.

Quick — turn back to PAGE 71.

The bear leaps at your back. You stop short, and it flies right over you. You turn to run, but a giant paw reaches out and grabs your leg. The claws tighten around you. The bear opens its mouth wide in a gruesome snarl. You pull with all your strength, but you cannot free yourself from its grasp.

Suddenly a shot rings out. The bear's grip loosens immediately. The bear staggers back, and you scramble away. The bear stumbles off into the woods, howling and moaning in pain.

You look up into the face of a man in a shaggy beard and worn, dusty clothes. He is carrying a large pistol. "Well, well, if it ain't the barn burner," the man says with a grin.

"Are you one of the settlers?" you ask, the fear showing in your voice, your leg still throbbing from your encounter with the bear.

Your question seems to give the man a big laugh. He is joined by two other shabbily dressed men, who have several horses tied up behind them — the horses from the settlers' barn!

"You — you're horse thieves!" you cry. "You're the ones who set that fire! You burned down the barn to steal the horses!"

The men just laugh at your words. "That's no way to talk to a man who just saved your life," their leader says to you. "Besides, we all know that *you're* the one who burned the barn. Then you pulled a gun on that kid back in the clearing."

"What are you going to do to me?" you ask,

trying to sound brave. You look around for a chance to escape as you talk to them.

"You might as well join up with us, kid," the horse thief says. "Those settlers are goin' to string you up, no matter what. You might as well take your chances with us. We're takin' these horses west — as far west as we can go."

"Well, that sounds interesting," you say, stalling for time. The nearest horse, you see, is within jumping distance. You could jump onto it and gallop out of there. What a daring escape!

But your leg is in pretty bad shape. And you're exhausted. Maybe you'd be smarter to take it easy for a while and play along with them.

If you choose to leap onto the nearest horse and try to escape, turn to PAGE 76.

If you choose to play along with the horse thieves for a while, turn to PAGE 80.

76

You take a deep breath and make your move. In one swift motion, you leap up onto the nearest horse and dig your heels into its side. "Ride, boy, ride!" you scream.

Too bad the horse was tied to a tree.

The thieves' laughter turns to anger. They reach for their pistols. You reach for the green pendant around your neck and squeeze it as hard as you can.

Nothing happens.

You squeeze it again.

Nothing.

Looks like you're not going to get out of this jam. The thieves are arguing over who gets to shoot you. You have one last hope. Daniel Boone. You saved his life. Now, maybe, he'll come to your rescue and save yours. Will he show up just in the nick of time?

Flip a coin.

If it's heads, turn to PAGE 84.
If it's tails, turn to PAGE 86.

Hot bear breath on the back of your neck is more than you've bargained for. Just as the bear leaps onto your back, you press the green pendant around your neck as tightly as you can. You close your eyes and pray that the pendant will work.

The next moment, you are happily climbing out of the Time Raider back in Uncle Edgar's lab. "Uncle Edgar," you say happily, "why are you so surprised to see me?"

The look of shock doesn't leave Uncle Edgar's face. "I'm *not* surprised to see you," he says in a trembling voice. "I'm just surprised to see that gigantic brown bear you've brought back with you!"

Seems as if your weary legs have got a bit more running to do. That bear looks mighty hungry! Time travel can raise a real appetite in *anyone!*

Better get those feet moving! Otherwise, this just may be

THE END

Your hand falls from the switch. "I'd better not pull it," you tell yourself. "There's no telling what it might do."

Instead, you reach up and grab at the green pendant. One squeeze and you will be back in the Time Raider. But your hand grabs at nothing but air. The pendant . . . where is it? It must have fallen off while you were running!

The guards grab you and lift you off the ground. They carry you to the tall, bearded man. "Who are you?" you cry angrily. "What do you want?"

"You do not know me?" he asks, surprised. "I am Dr. Chandon. You are not a robot, are you? You are a stranger here."

"You guessed it," you say. "Put me down."

"Are you a human by any chance?" Dr. Chandon asks slowly.

"Yes, I am," you say as the guards slowly lower you to the ground.

A broad smile breaks out on Dr. Chandon's face. He jumps into the air, a leap of sheer joy. "At last!" he cries. "A human! Another human! Thank goodness you have come to rescue me!"

"Rescue *you?*" you ask as he repeatedly slaps you on the back. "What are you talking about?"

"Look around," Dr. Chandon says with a broad gesture toward the crowded, frozen city. "All are robots. Everyone you see. Even my assistant and my guards. They are all machines! My government left me here in charge of them — and then abandoned me. You must take me with you! You *must* get me out of here, away from these robots! Please!" He grabs onto your shoulder, pleading.

"But I come from the distant past," you tell him. "I must go back centuries in time to my home. You might not like it back there."

"Anything will be better than the loneliness I've suffered here," he tells you.

Finally, you agree to bring him back with you. The two of you walk to the Time Raider. He never looks back once as he climbs into the capsule with you. As you begin to operate the controls, a wide grin creases his face.

You bounce and rumble back through time and land with a hard jolt back in Uncle Edgar's lab. "Sorry about that last bump," you say, turning to see how Dr. Chandon weathered the trip.

He didn't weather it very well. That last hard jolt caused his head to break off. Wires and electrodes spring out of his exposed neck. Dr. Chandon, it seems, is a robot, too.

Does this mean that the other people of the future city were humans? Or were they robots led by robots? Was *anyone* human in that city? Was anyone in charge?

You will never know.

THE END

"Well . . . I guess I oughta join up with you fellas," you say, trying to sound a little enthusiastic.

"Now, that's smart thinkin'," the leader says, clapping you on the back. "Bein' a horse thief ain't a bad life. You don't get a lotta respect, but —"

"Hey, wait a minute, Jedediah," one of the other thieves interrupts. "Have you lost your mind or somethin'? We don't need a kid taggin' along with us. We gotta make tracks. The kid'll only slow us down."

"You're right," Jedediah says grimly. "I wasn't thinkin'. We got no choice. Sorry, kid, but we gotta shoot ya. Them's the breaks. Do you want to shoot, Zeb, or shall I?"

Playing along with them didn't seem to help you out much. That horse is still nearby. Maybe you should jump on it and make a fast escape. Or, maybe it's time to squeeze the green pendant and get back to the safety of the Time Raider.

If you choose to escape on the horse, turn back to PAGE 76.

If you choose to squeeze the green pendant, turn to PAGE 85.

"I'm very sorry," you say, "but I juuust doooonnnn't seeeeee whaaaaaat Aaaaaaaaaaay caaaaaaaaan dooooooooo." You realize that you are beginning to slow down, too. Soon you are moving and talking at the same speed as everyone else.

Suddenly a group of people carrying all kinds of cameras, lights, props, and other equipment comes walking into view. They are walking and talking very fast. A man carrying a megaphone steps quickly into the middle of the street.

"Whaaaaaaat's gooooooooooing onnnnnnnnn?" you ask yourself.

"Okay, people, set up quickly. I want to shoot this street scene and get back by tonight. Come on — move, everyone."

He's talking so fast you can hardly understand him. He must be the tyrant from another planet. He looks like a movie director to you — and he is.

"I'm so happy I discovered this planet," the director says to his assistant. "I'm saving a fortune by shooting all my slow motion scenes here. These people move in perfect slow motion. Saves me millions on special effects!"

Congratulations. You're in the movies! Haaaaaaaave fuuuuuuuuuuuuuuun!

THE END

"Oh, I just couldn't play such a mean trick on Uncle Edgar," you say. "He'd never forgive me!" But your hand slips as you reach for the control panel, and you accidentally press the red button.

Immediately the Time Raider's quiet hum becomes a thunderous roar. It jolts forward, then back, then forward again, bouncing you back against the seat and then up against the control panel. "Ouch!" you cry, holding your head. "What's going wrong here?"

But now the time capsule is whirring you back through time. Lights glow and explode, and musical tones fill the capsule, then fade to silence.

The Time Raider lands softly. You peer out through the window. You can't see very well because the window has steamed up. You open the door to get a better look and find yourself in some sort of tropical marsh.

Gigantic vines have twisted their tentacles around the time capsule already, and the capsule has begun to sink into the soft, sandy mud beneath it. A bat with a wingspan as wide as a small plane hovers overhead, screeching and shrieking. Funny-looking birds, larger than any you've ever seen, walk along the ground, poking their noses at the Time Raider.

"Dodos!" you cry. "Just how far back in time have I come?!"

You don't have to wait long to find out. The ground seems to shake and the vines tremble as a giant creature approaches. "A dinosaur!"

you cry aloud. The batlike creature shrieks in reply and flies off. "Unbelievable! Now, what kind is it?" you ask yourself.

Trying to identify the dinosaur is a big mistake. You realize — too late — that you should be running from it instead! In seconds, it is upon you, lowering its head, opening its tooth-filled mouth, and . . .

You squeeze the green pendant around your neck. Do you escape? Turn to PAGE 88 to find out.

Daniel was heading home when he thought he saw another bear. It was actually some kind of evergreen bush, but no one told him that.

He's home hiding under his bed.

He'll be a real hero later on in life. But that isn't much consolation to you, is it?

THE END

You close your eyes and squeeze the green pendant as hard as you can. You can feel the air around you shifting and whistling. You are moving, floating. Your body is tingling strangely. Did the pendant work? Has it carried you back to the Time Raider?

You open your eyes. The horse thieves have disappeared, but you are still in the forest. You feel funny — heavy, lumbering, slow-moving, You look down at your arms. They are covered with brown fur. Your entire body is covered with brown fur!

You growl unhappily and scratch at your long, black snout. Obviously, there are still a few flaws in Uncle Edgar's invention. By squeezing the green pendant, you realize, you have changed bodies with the brown bear.

You swipe at the air with your paw. You sniff something. It's a kid walking through the forest. Your stomach growls. The kid will make a nice meal.

It's your old self that you see through your bear eyes. You begin to chase yourself, saliva dripping from your jowls, lumbering after yourself on all fours. What a roar you can make now! We never knew you had it in you.

Well . . . happy hunting!

THE END

That boy you saved back in the clearing wasn't *the* Daniel Boone. He was just some other pioneer boy with that name. The real Daniel Boone is off right at this moment forging a trail through the Kentucky wilderness.

The Daniel Boone you saved got eaten by the bear's mate on his way back to help put out the barn fire.

Amazing coincidence, isn't it?

Or perhaps the wonder of it all is lost on you, seeing the terrible situation it leaves you in. Tsk tsk.

THE END

Uncle Edgar climbs in. He's wearing his glasses and carrying his jacket. He begins to close the capsule door. "Wait a minute —" he cries. "Is that the phone ringing?"

"Who cares?" you scream. You press the button before he can open the door again, and the Time Raider begins to hum through time.

It doesn't hum for long.

The hum turns to a rattle. The rattle becomes a clanging. The clanging becomes a sputtering. The capsule begins to rock back and forth, the lights flashing off and then on and then off again.

"We may have problems," Uncle Edgar says, the concern showing on his face. "Big problems."

The time capsule is silent now, silent and dark.

With the machine in this condition, you have no choice but to turn to PAGE 91.

You are not back in the familiar safety of the Time Raider. Yet the dinosaur has disappeared and your surroundings have changed completely. You find yourself in an army camp. Mounted soldiers, armed with long rifles, seem to be preparing some sort of march.

"General Custer, we are ready!" a soldier yells.

"Wait a minute!" you cry. "Don't go!"

But no one hears you. The soldiers disappear. You find yourself on another battlefield. Jet bombers fill the sky above you. The sky is red and the air seems to be on fire. "Help me! Someone!" you scream, and dive for cover under a scraggly tree.

You don't reach the tree. Instead you find yourself floating on a platform high above a city of golden spires. A giant eel with two heads is talking to you. Both heads are talking at once, and you can't understand either of them. Suddenly, the eel become angry and shoves you off the platform.

You are falling, falling. You land inside a circle of people who are dressed as pilgrims. They are all staring grimly at a wooden stake in the middle of a pile of straw. You realize that you are being tied to the stake. A pilgrim approaches with a burning torch. "Help!" you scream. "Please! Get me out of here!"

Turn to PAGE 94, and keep away from those flames!

Uh-oh.

Didn't Uncle Edgar tell you never to push the white button?

How could he be so forgetful? Surely, he should have remembered to warn you against pushing the disintegrator button, since it causes the entire machine to blow up into tiny bits!

What a mess Uncle Edgar will find when he returns to the lab. Poor old guy. He won't even have you around to help him clean up — since you're part of the mess. Tsk tsk!

THE END

You may be trapped in a time warp. If you are, there is no escape.

Quick! Turn to PAGE 93.

"Hold on jest a minute," Daniel cries suddenly. The settlers stop a few yards away from you. "This stranger just saved my life. I was bein' chased by a b'ar an' this stranger frightened him into the woods with my rifle."

"Daniel, this stranger you are praisin' set fire to our barn!" one of the men yells angrily, taking a step closer to you. You back up a step.

"No!" Daniel says, his voice rising. He seems to gain courage by being the center of attention. "I saw the culprit what started the fire. It was thet b'ar. The b'ar knocked over a lantern by the barn door. When I started to warn ever'one, it took off after me. I saw the whole thing. This stranger is innocent!"

You are not only innocent — you are a hero for saving Daniel Boone's life. You return with the settlers and help put out the fire before it spreads to the cabins.

That night a big dinner is prepared in your honor. "I wish we could offer more, stranger," one of the settlers says humbly, "but this meal is the only reward we can give you."

He hands you a big bowl of steamy bear stew. One sniff tells you you've spent enough time back in pioneer days. You press the green pendant around your neck and return to the Time Raider, the pungent aroma of the stew still in your nostrils as you head off gratefully in another direction.

THE END

Nothing can warp the brain faster than a time warp.

Turn back to PAGE 91.

"Just stay calm. Don't worry about a thing." The flames have disappeared and you are looking up at Uncle Edgar. He is placing a cold washcloth on your forehead.

"I'm taking apart the Time Raider," he says with a smile that's intended to be soothing. "I'm dismantling it completely, so you don't have to worry."

"Dismantling it? Why?" you cry. You try to sit up, but your head hurts too much.

"Because it doesn't work, of course," he says. "What good is a time machine that doesn't take you through time?"

"But it *does* work!" you insist. "It just took me to prehistoric times, and to General Custer's army camp, and to —"

"What are you saying?" Uncle Edgar says, looking very concerned. "You haven't been anywhere. When that stupid machine started jumping around, you bumped your head on the control panel. You've been unconscious for about twenty minutes. The doctor said not to worry. It's just a concussion. He'll be back in a few minutes."

"But my trip back to —"

"You haven't been anywhere," Uncle Edgar says, taking a long look at the bump on your head. "Now, just stay calm. I'm tearing it apart right now."

You look over at the Time Raider. Was your whole trip just some sort of crazy dream? If so, how did those gigantic vines get tangled around the door to the capsule?

THE END